THE KISSING SCHOOL

SCHOOL

Sam Portland

Contents

Chapter 1-Oh Pardon Me Cameron, What Great Abs You Have

Stumbling down the hall way, I try to keep my steps quite so I won't wake up everyone else who is sleeping who are not being forced to go down to the kitchen to get a glass of water to wash down a nightmare. It's the same thing every time: the night my dad left. I've managed to stop waking up screaming, but still, I have to walk it off if I hope of getting anymore sleep for the night, and since it is only one o'clock, my butt is going back to bed or else!

Even though my senses are acute from having the heart-racing wake-up call and my feet have finally found a steady, straight rhythm, it is still really dark; so when I get to the steps at the end of the hall, I forget that there are three steps instead of two which leaves me sprawled out on the floor because of my miscalculation.

I lay there breathless as I listen to make sure my loud thump from my fall didn't wake any one up because I so do not want to explain this whole situation to anyone. Slowly, I crawl to my knees and eventually my feet. I can feel the welts rising on my knee and a little blood dripping down my palm. Great, all I can hope is that none got on the floor because I sure can't see well enough to clean it up.

Finally, I manage to make it to the kitchen without further damaging myself or my surroundings, but I just stand there like an idiot because I can't remember the layout of the kitchen sense they re-modeled it last week. Could this task get any more difficult? I feel like freaking Harry with the horcruxes! Alright this isn't going to be difficult, just find a wall. My hand connects with something hard, but its' weird. Do they make heated walls? Well, this is the twenty-first century after all. I run my hand up a little so that my hand is at a level where a light switch would normally be, but on the way up, the surface isn't smooth; it has deep crevices. What the heck? It's moving under my hand! I jump back, and by doing so, I land straight on my rump.

Light fills my vision, momentarily blinding me. Now my eyes and my butt hurt. This is the worst trip to get water ever. I think it's one for the history books. Just as I thought it couldn't get any worse, Cameron slowly fades into my vision as the momentary blindness subsides. Please tell me he just got here. He must have because if he didn't that means that I was rubbing his chest and no one has a chest that defined. Only models have chests that defined and half of them are air brushed.

The look on his face tells me that I did just rub my hand over his impossibly perfect chest. That's it I can't control my embarrassment any more as the blush lights up my face like a red light which only gets brighter when he loses control himself and his smirk turns into full blown laughter. At least his volume is able to shake me out of my daze, as I jump up and cover his mouth with my hand until he finally calms down enough for me to remove it.

Only now that it is completely silent, I feel the awkwardness of the situation slip in. I mean I just groped Cameron, my best friend's brother, in his kitchen. I can feel the blush sinking in as I scooch away from him and slide onto the nearest bar stool. Still neither of us says anything; we are just looking at each other. God, he is good looking. I mean it makes sense does make sense; Maria, my best friend, is drop dead gorgeous. Of course, anyone related to her has to be good looking, but he goes beyond good looking, he is a hot sexy ball of yumminess with his black hair that falls into his bright arctic blue eyes that are accentuated by a strong jaw line and a crooked nose that looks like it might have once been straight if it weren't for it being broken once or twice. Somehow that crooked nose only adds to his sexiness; probably because it shows that he doesn't really care enough to get it straightened like so many guys at our school. He's comfortable with who he is because he knows he is sexy as hell.

Cameron clears his throat, and I realize, like the idiot that I am, that I have just been staring at him. Great, he probably thinks that his little sister's best friend is some kind of freak. I open my mouth to say something to save myself from any more embarrassment, but no words come out. Now on top of staring, I'm popping my mouth open and close like an even bigger dunce; but what am I supposed to say 'Oh pardon me Cameron, but what great abs you have'? I think not. Cameron is bending over laughing silently, having to clutch his mouth to keep sound from coming out.

"Did you say what I think you just said?" His voice is choppy due to laughter, but it still comes out deep and silky.

"I didn't say anything." Yep. Play the innocent fool, and make him question his sanity! Genius, pure genius! Mwuah ha ha ha ha!

"Yes. You did. You said 'Oh pardon me Cameron, but what great abs you have.' I heard you very clearly Panda." At 'Panda' he starts grinning like a fool. I cannot believe he just reverted to using my childhood nickname!

"Most people call me Amanda now you know?" I shake my head, trying to put all blame on him. If the conversation focuses on my name, then we can all just forget about what I said about his abs.

"I'm not most people." He gives me another crooked grin and begins to walk away. Yes! I am free! No more embarrassing situations for me! Woot woot!

Just as I thought I was in the end zone of the most stressful football plays of my life, Cameron blocks my touchdown stopping me short of the five yard lie by stopping in the hallway between the kitchen and living room doors. He doesn't turn around all the way away, but he tilts his head just showing me that beautiful profile of his.

"And for future references Panda, you can run your hands up and down my 'great abs' any time you like." With that and a final chuckle, he walks into the living room and out of my site, but a soft glow coming from the T.V. reminds me of his presence.

I cannot believe he just said that! It takes me a whole ten times of counting to fifty to calm down enough to get the water that was the original purpose of this late night endeavor. After chugging down two whole glasses, my heart has finally stopped trying to beat its way out of my chest which helps me to breathe easier.

That was the most I have been around Cameron since we were kids. I mean yes I spend practically every day in his house, but we never really crossed paths. There was a hello here, a see you there, and what's up every once in a blue moon.

I wonder if he meant that I could run my hands up his abs any time; because if he was serious, I might just take him up on that offer right now.

Then it hits me like a ton of bricks: he was playing me for the fool that I am. He knew that that would get my hormones a boiling; that's exactly why he said it because he knows how to get under a girl's skin. Two can play that game.

Slipping off my long sweat pants that I pulled on before I left the room, leaving my long legs exposed in my soffe shorts, and my night shirt, revealing my tight tank top that my boobs are practically asking to be realized from, I check myself out in the mirror. Damn I am fine. My blonde hair is in a sexy disarray around my face, and there is a mischievous twinkle in my dark green eyes. Then I let my eyes wander down my body. My body is tight; there is no denying it. I run every morning, and work out every night, and do cheer practices and work outs five days a week on top of that. My muscles are firm and present, but not in a creepy, I'm a circus freak woman kind of way. Licking my lips so that they glisten, my final touches are done. I'm ready to go mess with one cocky boy's head.

I saunter—that's right saunter, not walk—into the living room where Cameron is sitting. All I can see is his head because he is facing the T.V. with his back to the door. That's fine with me one extra second to prep; making sure I'm giving this everything I have, I roll down my soffe shorts waist band so that my butt is practically falling out and a thick strip of my stomach and lower abdomen is now exposed. Just making sure, I get his full attention, I roll up my tank top so that it exposed my pierced belly button which no one knows about, but according to Maria, boys go crazy over. Here goes nothing.

I'm standing directly behind him, and he is so engrossed in some stupid movie on the television that he doesn't feel me standing there. That's just not acceptable sweetheart. I walk around the couch and stand directly in front of him. His mouth drops open as his eyes rake over my body. There we go; that's the attention I deserve. I squat down and run my hand up his outer right thigh, letting it rest there for a moment as I look into his eyes and lick my lips before reaching over and grabbing the remote to mute the television.

Before I know what he is doing, he pulls me down on top of him so that I'm straddling him; his hands never leaving my hips.

"Amanda what are you doing?" His voice is husky as all get out. Can you say 'turned on'?

Running my fingers lightly up and down his chest, I say, "You said that I could run my hands up and down your body any time I wanted." I see him take a big gulp and struggle to say something witty back. I keep running my fingers up and down, waiting for him to respond.

"I said chest." Oh crap, he did. Play dumb, I mean he is having issues thinking as it is.

"Hm?" I can see some strength coming back to him now

"Chest. I said you could run your hands up and down my chest not my body."

Giving him a coy smile, I let my fingers roam over his arms and legs. "Well maybe I adjusted the sentence to fix my wants." That sounded so stupid, but he bought it. His hands move from my hips up my back, and that's when I freeze.

"What? Why'd you stop Panda?" He knows I hate that nickname! That's it. Now I'm really going to mess with him. I shake my head, signaling nothing is wrong. He gives me a curious look as if he doesn't believe me, but he is now distracted by my hand which is roaming up and down his chest, dangerously close to the top of his pants. I hear him take in a quick breathe, and all my strength is being focused into not smiling. Lowering myself onto his lap a bit to get more comfortable, I feel something greet me. Are all guys that big? I swear, I don't know how his zipper isn't breaking. Slowly, I begin to grind our crotches together, and if it's possible his pants get bigger. I think I got him just where I want him.

He goes to run his hands up my shirt, but I stop him when he touches my hips. Grabbing his wrists, I move them back onto the couch and away from my body.

"Let me touch you Amanda." His voice comes out deep and extremely husky.

Hearing him say my name makes chills radiate throughout my body. Who knew my name could sound so sexy? Alas, I must not succumb to the temptation that is Cameron. I'm here messing with him for once, and I have him just where I need him to land the low blow.

"You might have said I could touch you Cameron, but I never gave you any such permission." Giving him my best slut smile, I begin to start tracing the contours of his chest again. I really should stop this because it is getting hard to focus on the task of getting even with him. Instead, I can't help thinking what those abs would look like without a shirt covering them. Because I'm lost in thought, I am not paying close attention to Cameron, so I miss it when his hands slide up under my shirt making their way to my bare back. I arch my back in appreciation of his hands, but then I realize what is going on. Cameron is touching my bare back with his hands, his hands! I jump off of his lap so fast it makes me a little dizzy, but I quickly regain balance and begin walking towards the stairs.

I hear Cameron behind me. "What the hell Panda? Where are you going?" His hand is wrapped around my wrist, but I shake him off and head back to Maria's room. "I told you that you couldn't touch Cameron. You touched. I walked. Goodnight." With that I walked away, leaving an awestruck Cameron behind me.

If I'm being honest with myself though, I had to walk away when I did because if I didn't things would have gone way too far, and trust me I would have let him go way too far. I had to stop because my planned backfired on me. Cameron wasn't the only one turned on. Then again, I've been in love with him for my whole life. What did I expect?

Chapter 2--Morning After

C hapter 2

I never thought that the clock would strike seven a.m., but when it did, I was out of the bed so fast it would make a sane person's head spin, but seeing that I've been up since one, I can no longer be considered sane. I head downstairs in the clothes I attempted to go back to sleep in which in turn were the same ones I was wearing when I had my little run in with Cameron in the living room.

You know that saying, 'don't do things at night that you'll regret in the morning?' Yeah, I wish I would have remembered that last night because I have some severe regret going on right now. Without even meaning to, I am in the kitchen and starting breakfast. Cooking always calms me down, so I hope everyone wakes up hungry because my hormones are in full throttle and I'm not sure just plain jane scrambled eggs will fix them.

I just put the last of the waffle batter into the waffle iron, topped off the eggs with shredded cheese that needs to melt, and now I'm starting on the bacon. It only takes a second before the savory bacon aroma is filling the whole house. How do I know this, you ask? Well, I'm a genius, and maybe because the scream from upstairs alerted me to Maria being awake, and she might have screamed something about bacon. I'm still leaning towards the first one though.

I hear quick footfalls on the stairs, and I turn around just in time to see Maria happy face standing in front of me. She comes towards me, acting like she wants a hug, but I know better. I point the fork I'm holding towards the table and give her a stern look. "No bacon until everything's done, Maria."

"Awe come on Amanda, I just wanted a hug!" I open my arms, but she fakes left, grabs a piece that I had sitting on a napkin, and off she goes, knowing she better run or suffer my wrath.

I'm so engrossed in flipping the bacon, checking the eggs, and waiting for the exact moment when the waffles turn the perfect shade of golden brown that I miss two people joining me and Maria in the kitchen.

"Mmmm. What smells so good?" I jump about a foot, forcing my back to be pressed into Cameron's shirtless chest.

"Take a chill pill Panda. I didn't mean to scare you." I hear Maria and Timothy, his friend who spent the night last night, laugh behind me. I just shake my head and attempt to move away, but Cameron has a firm grip on my waist. His lips gently brush my ear as he breathes huskily on my neck before pushing me back towards the stove.

"So, what's the occasion?" Cameron asks as he picks up a piece of bacon despite me battering him with my fork. Before I can respond, Maria pipes up.

"Did you not sleep last night? I felt you get up around one, but you never came back in the room." I can feel my cheeks heating up just thinking about what I was doing around one o'clock this morning, but only Cameron and I know what happened no one else. Thank goodness.

"No. I woke up and went to the guest room. I didn't want to bother you." Maria shakes her head in concern, but that's all I see on her face before turning around to remove the waffles from the very hot waffle plates.

"Is the same nightmare again?" My body goes stiff all over. I cannot believe she is bringing up my nightmare with the guys in the room. What the hell is wrong with her? Her and I both know where this conversation leads, straight to her telling me I need to go to a shrink to try and resolve whatever keeps these nightmares coming back.

"No. I just had a lot on my mind." I lie through my teeth, but I only feel a tiny bit guilty. She knows better than to mention the nightmares because I hate talking about them with anyone. It took me almost a year to tell her about them.

"Okay. I'm going to go shower before I eat. I'll be back in a bit."
Turning, I see her exchange a glance with Timothy before prancing
up to her room. She and Timothy have been sleeping together behind Cameron's back for about a month now. They aren't serious
about each other. They just like to have together, and right on cue
Timothy claims he needs to call his mom and climbs up the stairs,
answering the booty call he just received.

Turning back around, I silently chuckle to myself. Cameron is so
daft. How could he not see what was going on right under his nose,
his sexy nose. As I'm pulling the final pieces of bacon from the frying
pan, I feel a body press against me from behind. I can feel every inch
of Cameron behind me, and oh, did he feel good. His head is resting
on my shoulder as I cover up the bacon, not even trying to push him
away.

"You couldn't sleep, huh?"

I just shake my head 'no'. I sure can't trust my voice because I know
it would be a traitor and let Cameron know how turned on by him I
am.

"I couldn't sleep either even after an hour long cold shower, might I
add." His voice has an edge to it, but I can tell that he isn't angry, just
annoyed. Well if he is annoyed now, let's see how annoyed I can get
him.

Pressing my butt back against his happy stick, I feel him stiffen in
every sense of the word. Cameron flips me around and sets me on the

counter. Now, a normal girl would open her legs and let him push himself against her. Me? I cross my legs and swish my feet back and forth. The look on his face is priceless. He is beyond pissed off as he is tapping my leg trying to get me to open them, but I won't. Finally, losing all patience, he wraps one hand around each leg and forces them open, pulling me to the edge of the counter in the process. His lips are moving closer to mine, and I can see the pure lust in his eyes and something more, but I don't have time to analyze. I have to stop this kiss, and I do it the only way I know how by turning my cheek.

"Amanda."

"I'm sorry Cameron. I just..I just...I can't." His fingers pull my chin towards him so that I have to look at his gorgeous eyes that are shaded slightly darker than normal.

"What is it? Why can't you?"

"Promise you won't laugh?" He just nods his head in response. Some of the arctic coloring is coming back into his eyes. Good. He is calming down just as my pulse is taking off.

"I, uh, I have never really kissed anyone before." I could have sworn he was going to laugh; instead he looks like he is about to start yelling.

"Don't bullshit me Amanda. I know you have two ex-boyfriends, and the way you were acting last night and just now is not the way someone who has never been kissed acts."

I run a hand through my hair, at a loss for words because I really never had a real kiss before. Don't get me wrong. I have done the whole peck on the lips thing, but never have I used tongue, ever, and yes, I still possess my V-card which is hard to believe since I'm the head cheerleader. It's true though. Last night, I don't know what I was thinking. I wasn't. Something else had taken over my body is the only reasonable explanation I have come up with because I don't know what I was doing. I've never been that big of a tease before in my life. So what do I tell Cameron? I wouldn't believe me if I were him, especially with the way I've been acting, but I go for it anyway, hoping he'll believe me.

"So, you're telling me you've never made out with a guy?" I shake my head no. This is probably his fiftieth question, and all he is doing is pretty much asking me the same thing just in different terms. I think he believes me, but he is struggling to swallow it. Quick as a whip, his confused expression is gone and a look of complete satisfaction comes over his face.

"Well, we can fix this."

"How?"

"I'll French kiss you right now. Then that'll be another thing you can say you've done!" He begins to move in closer to me, but I stop him once again.

In the smallest voice I can muster, I ask him my deepest fear. "What if I'm not good?" At that he begins to laugh, until he realizes I'm being completely serious.

"That's impossible, of course you're going to be a good kisser."

"Don't say that. I know people can be bad kissers. Maria has told me all about it." Cameron just shakes his head, biting his lip. What is he thinking? Is it a complete turn off that I'm this in-experienced? Not that I want him to be turned on since he is Cameron, my best friend's brother, but still.

"I'll teach you. We'll meet up every day, and I'll teach you how to kiss. I'll also teach you what guys like and what not. I mean if you w-." I cut him off by giving him a bone crushing hug. This is perfect! Now I'll know if I am doing it right or not, and I won't have to stress about whether or not he likes it.

"I'll take that as a yes?"

"Yes!" I shout in his ear, and he ends up backing away a bit as if it really hurt, which it probably did. I hear footsteps in the hallway. Crap, I'm not done talking to Cameron yet. He has to teach me a lot.

"Where's your cell phone?" He asks in a hurried whisper.

"Upstairs. Why?" With a devilish grin, he runs out of the room to I can only assume get my phone. Just as he is leaving, Timothy walks in followed a minute later by Maria. Nice timing guys, no one would have ever guessed you guys just did it. Not.

I'm setting the table with all the food when Cameron runs back in a little out of breath. Every one gives him a crazy look, but no one questions it as we begin to eat.

Climbing towards the guest room where I slept last night to fetch my phone, I have a small knot in my stomach. Throughout breakfast I didn't get to ask Cameron what he was doing up here, and afterwards everyone shooed me out of the kitchen so I wouldn't help clean up since I cooked.

Finally, I grab my phone off the nightstand. I scroll through the contacts looking for Cameron's name in the C's, but it's not there. I could have sworn he came up here to put his number in my phone. On a hunch, I keep scrolling through all my contacts, and that's when I see it right there in the W's. Cameron had saved his name in my phone as 'What Great Abs You Have.'

He must think he is so funny, but somehow I can't bring myself to change it. I'm about to turn off my phone to conserve the little battery I have left, when a text message comes in from 'What Great Abs You Have' himself.

Kissing school starts tomorrow at five at the abandoned mill. Just FYI, the teacher doesn't like to be kept waiting.

Well, teacher, A.K.A., 'What Great Abs You Have', A.K.A , Cameron, A.K.A., my best friend's brother, tomorrow should be one hell of a lesson.

Chapter 3--Lesson Initiated

Chapter 3--Lesson Inititated

Riiinnnnng goes the bell, beckoning us to come to lunch. Even though I get straight A's, am a cheerleader, and participate in various clubs, that doesn't mean I like lagging after class when I could easily be enjoying the light banter that lunch time brings.

As I'm walking down the hall, I am searching for one black head of hair, but I don't see him anywhere. I have to admit that I'm nervous about today after school. I envy those girls who get their first kiss in an unexpected manor, but I can't be like them. I have to know that I'm getting my first kiss after school which only means that the butterflies I woke up with this morning are only multiplying in my stomach by the hour. If they were to cut me open right now, I'd have enough butterflies to fill a whole garden at the zoo.

When I reach the lunch room, I head towards the jock table without a second thought. That's where all of my friends sit; it just so happens that all my friends happen to be football players and cheerleaders. Generally, you befriend those you spend the most time with. Granted, half of them are complete idiots while the other half of them are complete assholes, leaving only one sweet, honest, true person: Maria.

She got to lunch first today, so she bought us both lunch. I hate when she gets here first because all our food consists of healthy things like salad or tofu. Yuck. I much prefer the days I buy when lunch consists of greasy, yummy in my tummy food. It's not like either of us needs to eat healthy, especially Maria. She's a stick. No, she's thinner than a stick. She's a twig! I'm sorry if I like my curves that come by eating high amounts of fat and sugar.

"What's up Amanda?" Johnny asks me from the other side of the table. I didn't even realize he is sitting there. Oops. Even though he is my boyfriend, I never even notice when he is around until someone points it out. Poor guy, he is so engrossed with me that he doesn't even realize I could care less about him. We did the brushing of the lips thing that one time at the movies, but I didn't feel anything so I refused to stay with our lips connected any longer. Now, I may or may not be avoiding his touch like the black plague.

"Nothing much Johnny. How was your weekend?" My heart sinks to a new low as he flashes me the brightest smile I have ever seen. Do I ignore him that much? Maybe I should try harder being his daunting girlfriend. Just wait sweetheart, after today I'll have my first real kiss out of the way, and we will be free to tango!

"It was okay babe. I missed you though." The butterflies in my stomach all come to an abrupt stop. The guilt I was feeling before was amplified now because he just said he missed me when I didn't even give him a single though. No, instead I gave a lap dance to a guy who screamed trouble and agreed to take kissing lessons from so said guy. I believe I just won the worst girlfriend of the year award. He doesn't deserve this. He is way too sweet for me. That's why I was telling him that we needed to talk before I even made up the decision to break up with him, but I knew then, when his face fell like I just broke tragic news that I had to break up with him because he is way too good for me.

Johnny and I agreed to meet after school at the local dinner to 'talk,' but we both know what is coming. Now, we are sitting in silence and I am just waiting for the words to come out, but I can't seem to form the right sentences to make this as painless as possible for both of us.

"I want to break up Amanda." I snapped my head up so fast that I think I might have pulled something because there is serious pain shooting up my neck now. Great, that'll be fun to deal with while I'm kissing Cameron later. Wait. No. Do not even think about Cameron right now. Think about Johnny. He just said he wanted to break up, but I could have sworn he was in love with me.

"Really?" The hope in my voice was inevitable no matter how hard I tried to hide it. We both know this is what I really want.

"No. Yes. I don't know." He takes a deep breath and his brown eyes meet mine. I never realized just how good looking he is before with his buzzed blonde hair and chocolate brown eyes and even though I can't see them now, I know he has a rocking six pack underneath that loose fitting blue polo.

"Look Amanda, I really like you, but I know you don't feel the same. As much as I wish you did, I know you never will. I can't be with someone who doesn't like me back even if I like her enough for both of us." With that he gives me a quick smile and stands up.

"I know you asked me here to break up with me Amanda, so I just wanted to beat you to the punch. If I let you do it, we might be here for another couple of hours." Giving me one last quick smile, he plants a light kiss on my forehead and walks out the diner door.

The relief floods through me as he pulls away in his run down 1972 Chevy truck. He is such a good guy. Starting tomorrow, my mission will be to find him an equally good girl that he can fall madly in love with, and she will love him back. That's the only way to fix the pain I just caused him because I'm such a heartless wench.

I wanted to like him. I really did, but I just couldn't bring myself to feel anything for those rich chocolate brown eyes. It's just that a little boy took my heart a long time ago, and he has yet to give it back. Plus, mom never raised me to be an Indian giver. If you give something to someone, you can't ask for it back. They have to give it back willingly, and he can't willingly give me my heart back because he has no idea I'm in love with him. And so the circle keeps on turning.

Glancing at the clock, I realize it is already 4:45. This is bad. Really bad. Being the rudest I have ever been in my life, I run straight out of the door, past the waitress without a second glance. Jumping in my Arcadia, I put the pedal to the metal and head towards the abandoned mill. It's at least a forty minute drive from the dinner, and I needed to make it in fifteen minutes. The minutes pass quicker than the miles did, and before I know it the clock strikes 5 when I am still a good ten minutes away.

I swear if that clock doesn't slow down and my speedometer doesn't speed up, I am going to go crazy! Just as I hit the outer edge of the mill's property, my phone starts buzzing. I glance about, looking for it, and debate on answering it. I mean, I'm already going 80 mph on this old road: dangerous enough. Then my phone stops vibrating and begins singing "I'm too sexy for my shirt. I'm too sexy for my shirt. I'm so sexy it hurts." I do not have that ringtone on my phone, or so I thought. Who could that be? Who put that as their ringtone?

While trying to navigate down the mill's massively long property, my curiosity gets the best of me, and I reach over to my phone and hit speaker.

"Where in the hell are you?!" Even though I have never talked to him on the phone before, I know its Cameron's anger that is springing from my phone's speakers. I make one last burst on my speedometer, and I come to a hurtling stop. I can see Cameron's car near mine, and it's a miracle I didn't hit it when I came to my stop. I'm not sure it's safe to drive like that. If my mom would have seen my driving like that, my cars, yes cars, would have been sold on autotrader.com in the blink of an eye. What mother dearest doesn't know, won't hurt her.

"I'm here. I'm here." I shout into the phone and at him, but it's not my fault I don't have my wits about me. I blame him. He shouldn't be this sexy. His hair is not in its usually perfect curtain around his face. The wind has seen to that. Strands are wrapped around his head, and it looks messy but sexy as hell. Then there are those eyes which I don't even want to get started on because if I look at them too long I might grow weak in the knees and fall at his feet which would be bad. I let my eyes roam down his face to his perfectly sculpted chest which was impeccably defined under that tight fitting white V-neck.

"You're late." One statement brings all those stupid monster butter-flies back again, but this time they brought friends and some family members along for the ride. He turns and stomps to the inside of the mill. I scurry in after him and begin o explain.

"I know. I'm really sorry. I just got caught up at the diner with Johnny." At Johnny's name, Cameron goes rigid all over, but he keeps walking. Why do I feel the urge to explain why I was with Johnny before meeting him? Finally, we reach his destination, a blanket covered in pillows in a well-lit corner. He throws himself down on the pile, and pats the area next to him.

Unlike him, I don't just plop down. I gently sit down, trying not to expose everything under my mini skirt. I tried to dress cute today by wearing a mini skirt that showed off the awesome legs I have from cheerleading and a tight fitting shirt with a sparkly design. I thought that I could pair it with some ballet flats and I would look cute, but not like I tied to look cute for him even if I did. Finally I'm situated in a slightly uncomfortable position, but that's what I get I guess for wearing a short skirt.

"We met to break up in case you were wondering." I look over at him as a flash of something crosses over his features, but it is gone before I can recognize what the emotion is.

"Are you sure you want to continue with this then? I mean we can just cancel if you don't want to anymore. I would understand." He has his face tilted down as he is saying all this. I really want to just crawl in his lap and kiss him all over. This position I'm in is really difficult to face him in. I jump quickly and startle him.

"Stay here, and don't move. I'll be RIGHT back!" With that, I run out of the mill and straight to my car. Digging through my gym bag in the back of my car, I find a pair of shorts and slide them on before pulling off my skirt. Not even bothering to lock my car since we are completely secluded out here, I run back in and fall down next to Cameron. His eyes rake over my body with a questioning glance, but if he noticed that I changed he doesn't say anything; instead, he goes back to looking at his lap like before.

Um, teacher? Aren't we supposed to be starting my lesson like now? How am I supposed to learn if you don't initiate something Cameron? Come on. Finally, I realize my mental pleas are useless, since he can't hear me. What to do, what to do? Should I just kiss him and go from there? Well, I could be a horrible kisser, and that could end badly. He is supposed to be the experienced one here! He should be doing something not sitting there being as useful as a lump on a log!

Being this close to Cameron, it is hard not to tackle him down and have my way with him even though I'm not really sure what my way is exactly. I'm a smart girl though, so I'm sure I could figure it out if he is unwilling to help me out. Our arms are about two inches apart, but I'm still hyper aware of how his body moves even if it is only a minor muscle twitch.

I cannot believe he is just sitting there! I can't take this anymore because this is on the verge of being riddikulus. We can't sit here all day! Taking the initiative, I slide up on my knees and crawl my way onto his lap. Once I'm situated, I sit down gently, crossing my legs out to the side while my arms are wrapped around his neck.

"Alright. I got this far. What next Mr. Teacher?" He laughs at me. Actually laughs at me! If he thinks that just because his laugh is one of the sexiest sounds ever that he can get away with laughing at me, he is so wrong. My anger is lost the second his fingers start caressing their way up my leg, landing on my hip which is where they stay.

"First lesson: the art of teasing." I can do this one. It'll be just like the other night in his living room. Give him just enough to leave him wanting more. However, even though I know a lot about teasing, I think I'm about to learn a whole hell of a lot more.

Looking directly into Cameron's eyes, I see how they are twinkling with the excitement of this lesson. I have a feeling I am in way over my head.

Chapter 4--There are Such Things as Bad Kissers

Cameron's eyes squint at me in concentration. Apparently, I am horrible at teasing. Here I was, thinking that I was a tease by trade, but no. I'm not. I suck.

"Amanda." He stretches my name out in a tight line. I think he is beyond frustrated, but I don't get what he is trying to tell me to do. His instructions aren't making any sense. If they were, I would be doing fine. This isn't really my fault here. He is all to blame, really; it's not me.

I let out a small whimper of apology, and he shakes his head. I'm glad this is lesson one instead of kissing. Imagine if I had to kiss him right now. If I'm this bad at teasing, I do not dare to think of how horrible I am at everything else.

"I just don't understand what you are trying to tell me to do Cameron. I'm sorry, but I don't get it." Cameron lets his head fall hard onto my shoulder. Is it possible to kill someone from frustrating them to death? I wonder if it is if it would be considered murder. I wouldn't think so. I'm not intentionally frustrating him. I tried to tell him this was a bad idea when we were in the kitchen, but no he was insistent. I can feel him physically brace himself before he leans back to look at me again.

"Just pretend that you want me to kiss you senseless, but you don't want to initiate the kiss. You want me to, so you are going to 'tease' it out of me by giving me just enough to make me want more. Try it. Try anything. You can't really go wrong here." He rests his back against the wall, looking at me expectantly. Leave him wanting more. Wait, I remember reading something in a magazine about this once. Something about barely kissing that drives people crazy. Bracing myself, I begin my first assignment.

Running my hands gently through Cameron's hair, I move my face closer to his. Starting at his ear, I make a trail of soft, barely there kisses right down to his jaw. Looking up into his eyes, I search for some kind of approval or disapproval, but I get nothing because his eyes are closed. Taking this as a good sign, I move my lips so that they hover over his. I breathe in and out deeply, letting my breath caress his lips before barely brushing our lips together. As I pull my face away, I take my hands out of his hair and lean back. The lustful look on his face tells me that I just passed my first quiz with flying colors!

Physically shaking himself, Cameron removes the effects of my teasing and comes back to his senses. He gives me an approving nod, but he doesn't utter a word as he just stares at me. His eyes bore in to me, and that look he is giving me is illegal, especially the part where he licks his lips. Does this boy know how he affects me? I mean, the only reason I am even doing this is because I've been in love with him forever, and I would sort of like him to be my first kiss. I know. I know. He is my best friend's brother, definitely in the no-no zone, but I can't help it. One look into those arctic blue eyes and I'm mush.

Lost in Cameron's eyes, I didn't realize our faces had moved closer together. Now our lips are mere centimeters apart, and my heart chooses this time to practice the tarantella. On instinct, the closer Cameron moves the farther back I lean. However, this only results in me losing my balance and falling backwards so I'm lying down. Not one to miss an opportunity, Cameron lies down next to me, forcing me to face the smile that is splayed on his lips.

"Don't be nervous Panda. We can stop our lessons at any time you know?" All words have left me. There is absolutely no way I can make any noises come out of my mouth. Even my mindless choking is gone now. Forcing my head to nod up and down, I finally act like a human with a brain, but it isn't my brain that is having the problem. My thoughts are working just fine. It's my tongue, and my vocal chords, and the rest of my body that is freezing up on me.

"Alright then. Lesson two: first kiss." First kiss? FIRST KISS? Why is he rubbing it in? I know I let it slip, but no one knows about it.

Not even Maria knows that! ARGH! This is bad, very bad. My body decides it's time to begin working again, and I start to shift uncomfortably. Even if Cameron notices anything off, he is ignoring it and plowing on.

"First kisses should be polite, sweet, and delicate. You want to leave the guy thinking you are an angel who has fallen down to earth to do nothing but bestow sweet kisses on him." I have to do all that with a first kiss? I don't even know how to kiss, and he expects all of this! He is ridiculous!

"Now sometimes, in a relationship, when it is time for the first kiss, the guy is expecting more: like tongue. However, do not go down that road. If he tries for tongue, he isn't worth your time. Got it?" I nod my head, smiling a big goofy grin. He probably thinks I'm crazy, but that's okay. He was talking about first kisses in a relationship, not for a person. This is fantastic! He probably doesn't even remember the part where I told him I've never had a real kiss.

"Okay. I'm going to walk you through my motions first, stopping before I actually kiss you. Then we will do it all over again, but faster and without my narration. Got it?"

"I think so!" Out of nervous habit, I bite my bottom lip while looking up into Cameron's eyes which are quickly growing darker by the second. Weird, that's almost the same shade they were that night in the—no. Do not think about that now. Letting out a shaky breath, I motion for Cameron to proceed with the lesson. He walks me through everything, and it seems pretty simple. All I really have to do is tilt my head in the opposite direction he tilts his and press my lips against his. That's it. He will do everything else

Taking a steadying breath, Cameron shuts his eyes before acting out everything he just said. Leaning into me, he brushes some hair out of my face and leaves his hand cupped around my cheek. Ever so slowly, he leans in closer and closer all the while sending sparks flying across my cheek as his fingers slowly caress it. If I thought my heart beat was going fast before, oh how I was wrong. That was nothing. There is no way that Cameron cannot feel that. It's like the bass at a hip-hop concert in there. My body is shaking with the beat. I swear it. Unaffected by my dangerously strong, fast, and loud heart beats, Cameron begins tilting his head and closing his eyes as he moves in closer and closer.

Alright, here it is: the moment of truth. Wait. What am I supposed to do? He told me I had to do something when he closed his eyes and began tilting his head! I know it was important, but I can't remember! UGH! If it weren't for the fact that he was so freaking close to me, I might remember, but I can't. Going on pure instinct, I close my eyes and let my body take over. The next thing I know, Cameron is pressing his lips against mine.

As soon as our lips meet, a heat spreads throughout my body, and I feel so alive. I just want to keep his lips there forever. I mean, people do that right? They kiss for hours on end. He is my teacher, and I do need the practice after all. All too soon, Cameron pulls away, but he doesn't just stop there, he stands up and begins walking away without a glance back at me.

"Cameron!" I scramble to my feet and run after him, but I'm too late. He is already backing out of the parking lot when I get out there. He just gave me my first kiss and ran like it was no big deal. See, I told him there are such things as bad kissers, and he just proved to me that I am one.

Chapter 4--He Wants to Play Me, but He is the One Who is About to Get Played

C hapter 4

The rest of the week passes in a blurry routine: get up, put on clothes, do hair and make-up, go to school, avoid Maria, play the role as if my heart is broken. When Friday arrives, I can't do it anymore. My façade cracks and I give up the effort I had been putting into acting like everything is a-okay. Today I wear my uniform, since it is a game, but my hair is back in a messy pony-tail with no make-up accentuating my pretty face.

The school is reacting to my appearance in a drastic way. People are pointing and whispering about me as I walk by. Luckily, they are owning up my raggedy ways to my recent break-up with Johnny, and since he is such an awesome person, he says he dumped me, thus giving me a reason to look like crap today.

I could take the stares and whispers, but what I cannot take is having to look my best friend in the face and lie to her about what's wrong. That's why I have been avoiding her, and it has been going really great for me thus far. However, all good things must come to an end. Barreling down the hallway, straight at me, is one very determined and pissed of Maria. Trying to make a run for it, I make it as far as the next set of lockers before she horse collars me, throwing me into the nearest classroom.

"What the hell is going on with you?" I forgot how piercing her screams can get when she is a little upset, but when she is pissed, they are lethal. My ears might be bleeding, so I go with the safest route and stay silent.

"Amanda! You hear what I said! Answer me dammit! You have been avoiding me like I have the black freaking plague, and now you show up to school like this! What in the hell happened Monday?" Looking at Maria, I can see the hurt plain in her eyes. She isn't just mad that I have been avoiding her. She is mad that I haven't seeked refuge in her friendship to solve my problems. If she only knew that going over to her house and sitting in front of the tv eating ice cream would only make everything worse, she would understand, but I can't make her understand because she would kill me or Cameron. My bet is on Cameron though. Sometimes I think she loves me more.

"I, I uh. I can't tell you." Not willing to look her in the eye, I find a very interesting tile on the floor and study it.

"Don't pull that 'can't tell you' bit with me missy. I don't care what you have done. Tell me what happened on Monday because you were fine with the break up with Johnny, but now you are acting all weird. What happened? Did he hit you? Rape you? Seek revenge on you for dumping him? What? Tell me!"

"No! Johnny didn't do anything! This has nothing to do with Johnny!" Shaking my head, I get some courage to look at her. Her pale skin has returned to its normal alabaster white. I might be safe to tell her the truth. I need to tell her the truth because what I really need right now is to form an "I Hate Cameron" club.

"It has to do with Cameron." Maria is off the desk so fast that I blinked and now she is in front of me. Who is she, Superwoman?

"What has he done now? Is he teasing you again?" I shake my head no and tell her everything from that restless night to him walking out of the mill after our kiss. Surprisingly, Maria stays calm through it all. There is no yelling, fuming, stomping, storming, cursing, muttering, or threatening. Well that is until I finish with my story; then there is all of that and then some.

Finally, I calm her down enough to get her to breathe at a normal rate. On the plus side, she isn't made on me. On the down side, it might not be safe for Cameron in his own home anymore.

"The nerve of that little bastard! How dare he do this to you? I have made it very clear to him that you are way more innocent than you look, and he is to not play his stupid little games with you. Does he listen? No!"

Shaking my head, I begin to laugh at Maria. The worst part is over. She knows the truth, and she isn't mad at me. I was so scared she was going to hate me for my stupid little mistake that I would lose my best friend. Silly me should have known it would take a lot more than getting my heart broken by her brother for her to disown me.

"Look Amanda, I get that he made you feel really shitty, but sweetie that doesn't mean you have to look shitty. Can I please fix your hair and do your make-up? Please, you look like crap." With those wonderful words of comfort, not, Maria begins to attack my face and hair with a vengeance like no other. After about twenty minutes of torture, she steps back with a happy look on her face.

"There, you look hawt! This will definitely make Cameron think twice about what he has done to you! If nothing else, he will regret not sticking with it longer to try and tap that!" Maria's comment has me bent over laughing. God, I love this girl. Thank you for sending her to me.

Not sparing myself a glance in the mirror, I jump off the desk, following Maria to the cafeteria. I'm not really sure what is coming over me, but I decide to switch up my normal behavior. Instead of walking my normal gait into the large filled cafeteria, I stop Maria and try out a new walk, waiting for her opinion of how I'm swinging my hips in a hopefully seductive manner.

"If I wasn't straight, I would totally do you!" Laughing, I lead Maria into the lunch room which goes silent as we enter. Everyone is staring at us, but I don't let it get to me. I know I look hot because of whatever Maria did to my face and hair on top of my newly found seductive walk. Coming to a stop in the cafeteria, I twirl around looking for that head of black hair who so wonderfully made me feel like shit. Maria with her sixth sense, figured out who I was looking for and helped in my search. Finally, we find him sitting at a long table on the far end of the cafeteria. His eyes are glued to me as I begin to slowly make my way over to him. Unfortunately, there are no empty seats at his table. What to do? I don't want to talk to him standing over him, but then again, he would get a nice view of my awesome legs if they are at his eye level.

"His lap. Sit in his lap." Maria's suggestion catches me off guard, but I love it for everything that it is. This will be perfect. He wants to play me, but he is the one who is about to get played.

Chapter 5 --That Shade of Milk Really Compliments Your Eyes

C hapter 5

Following Maria's beautiful advice, I slide my dairy-aire right onto Cameron's lap. To say he is shocked is an understatement. Rubbing my hand over his chest, I breathe softly against his ear as I move my lips down close to his. The silence that is surrounding us lets me know that I have the whole cafeteria's attention. My lips hover about a centimeter away from his when he begins to lean in to kiss, but I move my head quickly so I am back to his ear.

"What are you doing Panda?" His voice is husky and makes it really hard to think straight, but I push on. He will not win this round.

"Mastering Lesson 1." With that I stand up and dump a carton of milk on his already shocked expression.

"That shade of milk really compliments your eyes." Without giving him time to recover, Maria and I run out of the cafeteria and to her car. We aren't going to bother to stay for the rest of the day. What's the point? The only thing the students will be talking about today is what I just did. I feel a little bad from pulling the spotlight from the teachers, but not bad enough to take back my actions.

Broken giggles and sentences make up our entire conversation on our way back to her house. Neither of us can't stop laughing because just as we begin to calm down we will mention Cameron's face, hair, look, etc., and we begin laughing all over again.

Thirty minutes later

"Pick a movie already Maria! I am getting bored!" Sprawling out on the couch in front of the massive television, I make sure I am extremely comfortable for the movie extravaganza that we have decided to have.

"I got it! I'm coming, give me just a sec!" I hear her running upstairs to do whatever she is doing, so I close my eyes and relish in the day. Finally, I feel like I'm back to myself. What happened between me and Cameron isn't holding me down anymore. Yes, it still hurt like hell to think about his reaction to the way we kissed, but payback is as sweet as ice cream, and every girl knows that there isn't a problem that can't be cured by ice cream.

Mmm, ice cream—milk would be good right now. Wait, do I smell milk? Hm, must be Maria in the kitchen. That's what that door was.

Cuddling further into the couch, I begin to hum silently to myself. That's why I don't know anyone is laying in the room until they are laying on top of me.

Going with my first instinct, I try to wail my fists at the person on top of me, but Cameron easily pins my arms down with one hand. Looking up at him, I realize he isn't wearing the shirt that I soaked in milk toady. He isn't wearing a shirt at all, and the way he is slightly lifted off of me gives me a view of his oh so beautiful abs. Just as I am really enjoying the view, Cameron's pissed voice greets my ears.

"What the hell was that today Amanda?" I cringe at my name. Weird, I'm usually always wanting him to call me by it, but when he actually does, I hate it.

"What were you thinking? At first, I thought you lost your damn mind because you were openly flirting with me in school, but then you dumped milk on my head! What the hell?" His body is shaking which doesn't help with me not focusing on his gorgeous figure. Does this boy spend all of his time at the gym? I feel a little shake come from where Cameron is holding my wrists, and I snap back into attention.

"Payback is a bitch Cameron!" I don't know where that venom came from, and the look on Cameron's face told me he had no idea what I was talking about. Oh, boy. I sure will enlighten him.

"Remember the deal? You were supposed to help me, and I was scared of what would happen on my first kiss! That's why you were there because even if I was bad, you'd help me through it! You didn't! You just left!" The tears begin to slowly roll down my cheeks. I guess I didn't even realize how hurt I was when Cameron left until he was right in front of me. The way he just walked out on me is wrong on so many levels. I look at Cameron expecting him to be pissed at my sorry excuse, but I only find a saddened expression.

"Oh Panda, I didn't know that you thought that's why I left. I'm such an ass. I'm sorry." Wait? What? I'm confused. He is sorry and didn't know I thought that. Well, what was I supposed to think? He just left like it was nothing, like I was nothing! My inner rant is interrupted when Cameron places his lips against mine. It starts off as a gentle kiss, but it turns quickly into something more. He licks my bottom lip, asking for enterance, but I keep my lips sealed tightly shut. I'm no where near ready for all that to go down. Embarassing myself further in front of Cameron is not high on my list of things to do.

"Open your mouth!" Cameron's words are quiet by husky, and I know how bad he wants me to, but I can't consciously do it. I feel him grumble against my mouth as his attempt at licking my bottom lip fails him again, and just when I think I'm safe, he pushes our bod-ies together in every imaginable place while nibbling on my bottom lip. I can't help it; I moan. Seizing the opportunity, Cameron laces his tongue through my open mouth and begins to slowly caress mine. His hand is roaming over my leg, and he hitches it up and around him, pushing himself into me more. This makes me moan again, and I can feel the smile that is splayed across his cocky arrogant lips, but I don't care. This feels way too good to stop.

"What in the hell is going on in here?" Maria's voice makes us both freeze. We have totally been busted.

Chapter 6--Even a Pint of Ice Cream Couldn't Ease This Ache

C hapter 6

I push Cameron away with such force that he loses his balance, and since I wasn't smart enough to take my leg down from his waist, so I fall down right on top of him. For a girl who is supposed to be a graceful cheerleader, I do some pretty clumsy stuff sometimes. Managing to gain my composure, I roll off of Cameron and stand quickly, but he remains on the floor, covering his face with his hands.

"Answer me! What in the world did I just walk in on?" Me kissing your brother with a fiery passion? Foreplay? Hot make out session? Well, I'm not sure those are the answers she is looking for, so I just sit there with my mouth shut and wait for something to come to me or for her to disappear. I'm personally leaning towards the second one as my favorite, but lucky for us all, Cameron finds his voice.

"Timothy dared me to kiss her. He said that after that stunt in the lunchroom that I wouldn't have the balls to put her in her place. However, he was wrong." With that, he stood up and walked out of the room without a second glance at me. The words freeze me in my place and a pit grows in my stomach. Please, don't let it be true.

"Amanda?" Sitting on the couch, I just shake my head in silence. Why do I have to be in love with an asshole? It isn't fair. I mean, why can't I just hook up with one like Maria. At least she doesn't get hurt all the time. She just performs a hit and run, and she is good to go!

"Oh, Amanda." Maria wraps me into a large hug, but her words are drowned out. Stupid boy made my heart cry so loud that my ears no longer work.

Where God is that boy that I fell in love with all those years ago? I want him back. Please, give him back to me.

Sunday is a sacred time for most Americans, even those who aren't religious. Some people spend the day decked out in their team's colors, sitting in front of the largest television they can find in order to watch their team toss around the ole pigskin. Others spend the day resting up to prepare themselves for the week, so that when the ball gets rolling they will have the energy to keep pace with it. Some spend the day devoted to catching up with the family they so unwittingly neglect the other six days of the week. Others spend the day in worship and praise of the Lord, rejoicing in his name.

Today, I do none of those things. Instead, I opt out to lie in bed, basking in the misery that is my heart. The pain is constant and unmoving, even a pint of ice cream couldn't ease this ache. Maria tried to get me to stay, so she could comfort me. I just couldn't stand to be in the same house as him. It hurt too much, and it still does.

Someone once told me that you should cry your tears, and then just forget about them, forget about the people have caused them, forget about the events that bring them to your eye, and most of all, forget about the sadness in your heart. Tears should cleanse you of your pain and give you a fresh start. They wash away your past pains, giving you a fresh start on the day.

That mindset had always worked well for me, but I just can't manage to crawl out of this bed. I try, don't get me wrong. I pull the covers back, move into a sitting position, slide my feet on the ground, but when I go to put my weight on my feet, my knees go out, sending me spiraling back down right to where I started.

My whole body aches, and my head has gone into a fuzzy state from all this crying. I've never felt like this before, and I just want it to end. Rolling over, I notice someone entering my room, but I can't make them out—my tears are that thick. The unknown places a cold hand on my head before pulling it back as if I burned them.

"Oh, Amanda, you are on fire!" Maria? Oh, thank goodness it is you! Please make the pain stop. Please beautiful friend, make your brother's pull on my heart end, and with that my world goes black.

Two days later

"Amanda! Wake up!" Maria's voice is far off, so I'm ignoring it. This sleep is too good to miss out on. She'll understand.

"Amanda! I said, wake up!"

"uhhhhhhhhhhhhh!"

A fluffy object connects harshly with my face, causing me to sit upright which in turn makes my head spin from the quick action.

"About time! You have been out of it for two days!" I look at her curiously as I lay back down in the soft wonderfulness that is my bed.

"Why are you talking crazy Maria?" She shakes her finger at me while sitting down next to me. Oh joy, story time!

"Crazy? You have been asleep for two whole days Amanda! It's Wednesday. You've missed two whole days of school because you have been so sick. I came over Sunday because I hadn't heard from you in a while, and I find you lying in bed crying. Thinking that you were just balling over my idiot good for nothing brother, I went to put a comforting hand on your head, but you were so hot that it shocked me. Now, don't be mad—." Mad? Why in the world would I be mad? She came over to find me lying in bed with a fever so high that it nearly burned her?

"Don't be mad, but I called Cameron to come over. He is downstairs now actually."

"You did what?" I scream it so loud that it hurts my own ears, but I believe the reaction to be completely worthy of the statement! She better have a really good explanation for this behavior!

"I didn't know what to do, and he volunteers at the hospital sometimes! I didn't know who else to call! Please believe me! When I told him, he was really worried, and he came straight over! This is the first time he has left your side? I know that doesn't count for anything—believe me, I don't think it does either. It is just that—can't we let him have a little slack?"

"Slack? You want me to give him some slack? Do you realize that I have been in love with your brother for years? There is no slack here Maria!" Oh shit, did I just tell her that I'm in love with her brother? Risking a glance at Maria, I look up to find her giving me this great look of pity.

"I've known about your feelings for my brother. Why do you think I've been so adamant about you guys not getting together? Why do you think I only tell you about the bad stuff he does? I knew he would break your heart Amanda, and I didn't want to lose my best friend because my brother is an idiot who doesn't know how to have a girlfriend."

Maria gives me one last look of pure pity before standing up and leaving me alone in my thoughts. She has known about my feelings and has purposefully tried to deter me off my path, but I persisted. She was right though, he broke my heart. She was wrong though, too. She will never—I mean never—lose me as a best friend even if that means dealing with that wretch that she shares DNA with.

Cameron's POV

The scream sends chills down my body, forcing me drop the soup I was making and run upstairs. However, the scream has turned into heated words when I reach the door. Not being one to barge in on a private conversation, I turn to leave, but stop dead in my tracks when I hear Amanda's voice.

"Slack? You want me to give him some slack? Do you realize that I have been in love with your brother for years? There is no slack here Maria!"

The words are as sharp as the edge of a sword, and they sting just as bad. She has been in love with me for years, and I just did what I did. I was her first real kiss and love, and all I managed to do was break her heart. Like she said, there is no slack here. I have no excuse.

For her, it will be best if I just stay away. She deserves so much better than a delinquent kid who has had more experience than is good for him. I will make sure she moves on and finds someone who deserves her love because right now I don't. Even if I do love her back.

Chapter 7 --Instead of a White Horse, He Has a Black Motorcycle

C hapter 7

    "Die! Why won't you die you stupid zombie?" Pushing with all her might onto the controller, Maria tries and tries to kill the zombies on the game, but she continues to fail miserably. I gave up trying to play with her a while ago when all she managed to do was "accidently" kill me. See if I save her from the zombie apocalypse!

Her attempt at witty banter with the unresponsive screen gets a kick out of me, and eventually, she abandons the game to lay on the bed with me just giggling. That's how we stay most of the day. Just sitting there, giggling our butts off over the stupidest stuff. I have almost forgotten that Cameron is even here until he walks into the room carrying a bowl of soup.

His presence causes the laughter to die on my lips and my blood to run cold. Even though I did the whole crying thing over him already, seeing him still really sucks, especially since he is being really sweet by trying to heal me back to health.

Without a word to either me or Maria, Cameron places the tray of food at the end of my bed and walks right back out of the room. I can feel Maria's eyes on me, but I'm studiously ignoring her due to the fact that I have found a highly interesting string on the mattress. My ignoring her has nothing to do with the fact that I don't want to see the pity in her eyes. No, that can't be it!

"That's it! I can't take this anymore!" Maria is towering above me with her hand resting on her cocked hip. A cocked hip is never a good sign with her. It usually means that the fit is about to the shan.

"Take what?"

"This! You are feeling better right?" I nod my head slowly, slightly frightened of what those turning wheels of her are plotting.

"Good! Get up! We are going out!" Not giving me a chance to respond, she grabs my hand and throws me towards the shower, locking the door behind me. I guess this is the part where I willingly agree to be dragged to an overpopulated club filled with guys who see me as nothing other than a sex object because any girl in her right mind would willing subjugate herself to that!

****

"Maria you have five more seconds of pampering before I go back to bed in defeat!" I'm sorry beautiful friend of mine, but if I have to put up with one more second of you perfecting my look, I am going to explode. After my shower, Maria blow-dried my hair and insisted that I curl it. Then, I was incapable of doing my own makeup or picking out my own clothes, so she did those things for me as well. Now, she is standing before me, making sure all the final touches are in place. I understand that she is trying to be a good friend and help me get my mind off of a certain someone, but she is about to drive me crazy with all this straightening and fixing.

"Fine! I'm done! You are the object of perfection."

"Can we go now?" I let out a low whine and stand up. I don't even bother looking in the mirror because I don't care. I'm in a dress so short that my ass is in danger of falling out, and my hair and make-up is done to perfection because of Maria. Surely I look fine, or else Maria is one crappy friend which she isn't.

"Oh, stop complaining and get happy! We are about to party!"

I follow Maria's blue dress clad frame down the stairs and out the front door. Somehow we don't run into Cameron, but I'm not complaining—less time around him the better. We climb into the taxi that is pulled up to the curb. We both decided that either of us driving would be pointless because we both will be drinking. Just because we are drinking underage doesn't mean we have to do it irresponsibly.

"Where are we heading beautiful ladies?" The cab driver turns around, giving us a toothless grin. His eyes roam over our bodies, making me feel severely under dressed.

"Degree Zero: the club located on twentieth." Maria gives him a look that says 'You don't have a chance in hell so stop undressing me with your damn eyes.' A smirk makes its way to the creepers face before he turns around and sets off towards the club.

"Where are we going exactly?" I look over at Maria to see her texting furiously about something to the point where I don't even think she heard me. Oh well, I'm fine with that. I heard of the club before, but I've never been. There are some vague rumors over what the club is like. I heard that you are given mink coats when you walk through the door, but they aren't regular mink coats. They're somehow still revealing and sexy which I don't get. They are mink coats. What's sexy about that? Another thing I heard is that everything is frozen inside to the point that you have no choice to dance the night away or you will freeze, and by dance the rumors mean practically have sex. Whatever it takes to keep the body heat up right? No, that's disgusting. Sorry rumor mill, but I'm not grinding on everyone in the club just to stay warm.

The taxi rolls to a stop outside of a large warehouse with a long line of people outside, and by long line, I mean wrap around the block kind of long line. These four inch heels are too damn high to be standing in line all night long in order to go inside for a few hours and get groped and man-handled by a bunch of too touchy drunk guys.

"Are you just going to sit there, or are we going to go into the club?" Maria's voice floats over from the other side of the cab. You could say she sounds completely irritated.

"Have you seen the line?"

"Have you seen your legs?" Flipping around, I give her a confused look.

"Explain." Sighing heavily, Maria climbs out of the cab. My eyes follow her as she sashes around the cab, grabbing almost every man in line's attention while she makes her way to open my door.

"Get out Amanda. We aren't waiting in line. We are the definition f*ckable tonight, so get your butt out of that cab and to the bouncer, now. Work your hot girl charm and get us into this club." She sends me a small smirk, holding out her hand. I look at it warily, but eventually, I grab it and slide out of the cab.

I pull down my dress which hiked up slightly while in the cab before heading towards the front of the line. The bouncer spots us when we are a few feet from the front of the line. He is about to let in a group of twenty something scantily clad girls, but re-clips the hook on the line when he spots us. He is good looking, there is no denying it. The black shirt is about a size to small and hugs his very impressive muscles in all the right ways. His short blonde hair is spiked out in every direction in a really sexy way that somehow manages to highlight his gorgeous green eyes. This at least won't be a disgusting nasty bouncer who I have to press myself against.

Walking up to him, I press my body fully against his in all the right places, letting my hand run slowly over his chest. Snaking his arm around my waist, he gives me a small smirk. He would be lying to anyone if he said he didn't love his job. Boy probably gets laid easier than the bartender.

"Can I help you?" He jerks me closer to his body which somehow fits perfectly with me. I feel a slight tingle in my stomach when he smiles down at me.

"Let us in." I feel his hand playing with one of my curls, letting his hand slowly rub up and down my back.

"What's in it for me sexy?" His voice his husky in my ear, and I smile up at him, knowing he is already going to let us in.

"A dance with me later." Without releasing his grip on my waist, the bouncer unhooks the line blocking the door to let me and Maria in.

"That better be one hell of a dance." He lets his hold on me weaken, but I pause for a second before stepping away and into the club after Maria. I swear bouncers are so easy. Sometimes it is like taking candy from a baby because it is nothing but empty words. Girls promise them sex, but it is very rare anyone follows through. I get into the club, and he doesn't get laid. Win for me. Lose for him. I'm not losing any sleep over it though.

The temperature drops a significant amount when we walk through the door. It isn't uncomfortable, but I'm not all warm and cozy either. I make my way to the bar where Maria is to find that she has ordered us two shots in frosty looking glasses. We both take the shot at the same time, slamming the now empty glasses upside down on the light blue bar.

"Again!" The bartender slides us two more shots, and we repeat the process before ordering two regular drinks called something that's related to ice. I don't pay attention to what the bartender says. I just focus on the feeling of release I'm getting as the alcohol is seeping through my pores. Tonight is going to be a good night.

"Let's dance!" I grab Maria's hand, dragging her behind me to the crowded dance floor. I let my body move to the music ignoring the bodies that are pressed against me in this cramped space. I just let the rhythm move me in a way that I can never let happen in cheerleading. It isn't structured enough for our routines, but it's coming to the club and getting to dance like this that reminds me how much I love cheerleading and performing in front of crowds. Letting my body take over every cubic centimeter of my brain that is screaming that this will be a bad idea, I climb up onto the stage next to the DJ and dance like never before. Granted, some of the moves aren't exactly PG, but the screaming dance floor doesn't seem to mind too much.

I spot Maria in the crowd, grinding against some twenty-something who looks like a total dirt bag, but I ignore that because she looks like she is enjoying herself. Of course she is, she is practically having sex on the dance floor. Why wouldn't she be having a good time?

A guy near the front of the stage grabs my attention, but not in a good way. He has his eyes locked in on me as he moves closer to where I am. Looking me up and down slowly, he licks his lips in a disgusting manner. I take a step back away from the edge of the stage, but he doesn't get the message. He keeps moving closer. Now he is right underneath me, giving me a smirk. Somehow, the smirk reminds me of Cameron, but where Cameron's smirk is pure sexy, this guy's smirk is scary as hell.

What would Cameron do in this situation? Kick his ass for looking at me? No, why would he do that. Remember, he isn't interested Amanda. You are a big girl. You can take care of yourself. Plus, you are in a club full of crowded people. It's not like he can do anything to you.

"Hey sexy!" His voice radiates upwards, and I can smell the alcohol on his breathe all the way up here. I ignore him and keep on dancing to the beat.

"Hey! I'm talking to you!" I glance down quickly at him, but once again my eyes are glued to the rest of the crowd, ignoring him. Unfortunately, he won't be shot down this easily. I hot, sweaty presence wrap around my ankle, looking down I see a hand that is attached to, you guessed it, the creepy guy.

I shake my leg, but he won't loosen his grip. I give him a look trying to communicate that I wasn't in the mood to deal with his shit, but he obviously doesn't get it because he only tightens his grip. Okay, in the beginning, this was just annoying. Now he is actually starting to hurt me.

"Let go!" I squat down and try to pull his hand off of my ankle, but it is to no avail. He won't loosen his death grip on me. I can feel his hand sweat begin to run down my ankle. That is completely disgusting. Just let me go jerk-face. See what he is making result to? I just used jerk-face as my name-calling device.

"No! I saw the way you were looking at me. I know you want me, so why don't you come down from there, and we will get a room?" I freeze in my movement, and just stare at him. He can't be serious. I don't even remember looking at him, and if I did, it wasn't for long enough to make him think that I want to sleep with him. This guy is not only drunk but delusional—fantastic, just fantastic.

"Let go of me! I am not interested!" We have gotten a couple of people's attention, but he none is stepping in to help me out. Are all good Samaritans dead, or just not going to this club? Well I guess a good Samaritan probably wouldn't be going to a night club. I'll settle for a nice guy! How about a nice guy? Nope, okay everyone in this club sucks. I look around the room again, trying to find Maria for help, but I don't see her anywhere. Just as my eyes are making their way back to the creeper, I feel his hand being ripped off of my leg which causes me to stumble a little, making me fall off the stage. I feel my feet going out from under me, and I brace myself for the drop that is to come, but it isn't as bad as it should be. I only feel collision on my back and my knees, and that's it. Opening my eyes, I see the bouncer from earlier holding me in his arms.

"So, how's life?" I can't help it. Those simple words make me go into hysterics because of the whole situation. I feel his chest vibrating against me as he laughs along with me.

"Not much, just chilling." I manage to finally choke out. He smiles down at me, and my body can't help itself. Butterflies fill into my stomach.

"Want to get out of here? I just got off." Smiling up at him, I nod my head. I expected him to put me down, but he doesn't. He carries me straight out of the club: past the creeper, laying on the floor; the curious gazes of fellow club goers; the current bouncer who doesn't even question the situation; and the line of people outside waiting to get into the building. I thought that after all that he would put me down, but still he carries me around the building as if it isn't a big deal. He isn't even breathing heavily. He comes to a stop in front of a shiny, black motorcycle that is resting against the curb of the alley behind the club.

"I'm going to put you down now okay?" He slides me down to my own two feet, but he keeps me pushed against his body, no room existed between the two of us.

"You got a name Ace?" I cock my head at his nickname for me, but I still smile as I tell him my name. He gives me a smirk before untangling himself from me and climbing on his bike.

"Well Ace, you getting on?" Looking back at the club, I think of the creeper lying in a heap on the dance floor. It's because of this guy in front of me that situation didn't go farther than it did. Then, there is Maria who is currently dancing with some guy inside the club if she hasn't left with him yet. She is going to leave with him eventually; I saw the look she was giving him. Thinking of Maria, I can't help but think of Cameron and his smile and eyes and sexiness. Bouncer is good looking, not as good looking as Cameron, but he is definitely hot. Plus, he was there for me when I needed him without even really knowing me. He is a modern day Prince Charming, but instead of a white horse, he has a black motorcycle. I am trying to get over Cameron, and I don't see any better way to do it than jump on the back of this guy's motorcycle, so that's what I do.

Throwing my leg over the motorcycle, I try and straddle it the best I can without showing anything to anyone we pass by. I wrap my arms tight around his waist, feeling his taught muscles under that black shirt.

"So do you have a name?" I whisper in his ear as he turns the motor over. He pulls up to the street and revs the engine. I don't know if he can hear me, and I am about to repeat myself when he juts out onto the street, forcing me to tighten my grip on me. Just as I give up on learning his name, he tilts his head sideways and shouts.

"Damien!"

Chapter 8- Rule Number 4: Don't Do It Against Something That Can Move.

C hapter 8

Damien flies down the highway, slowly making his way out of the downtown district towards the suburbs on the other side of town. Some part of me is screaming, telling him to stop his bike. I don't know him, and this isn't safe. He could be a complete psycho for all I know. Then, there is the hormonal drunk teenager part of me that is currently feeling his rock hard muscles that are rippling under my hand; that part of me is saying that this is all perfectly fine. I mean, he did save me from the club creeper. How bad could he be?

The bike is slowing down, and I notice we are coming to a stop at a red light. I feel him place his hand over mine which is on his stomach.

When our skin touches, I get this tingling feeling throughout my whole hand that radiates up my whole arm which only gets worse when he links his fingers with mine. Unfortunately, it all ends too soon when the light turns green and he has to take off, leaving my hand suddenly very cold.

Luckily, we are still in a semi-populated district with lots of stop signs and red lights. Like at the last red light, when we come to a stop, Damien takes his hand of the handle bar of his Harley to link it with mine. I begin anticipating his touch the second we begin slowling down, and It is nice to be rewarded with the warm sensation when our hands connect again. It feels nice to have our hands connected like this.

Without meaning to, I let my mind drift to the way I feel when Cameron is touching me. When our skin brushes, even for a second, it is like pure electricity is running through my very core. The way his lips and body feel when pressed against me; the mere thought of it leaves my cheeks red. Without realizing it, I've managed to pull myself dangerously close against Damien; there is no room between our bodies now, and in the process of getting into this wonderful position, I have thoroughly managed to let my dress hike to above my butt, exposing my lacey black panties which I probably wouldn't have noticed if it weren't for the wolf whistle coming from the black Mustang that pulls away before I get a good look at the drive and passenger who looks strangely like—no that couldn't have been him. Standing slight, I pull down my dress and situate myself back down on the bike with a little bit more room between me and Damien. The second my arms wrap around his waist again, we are off.

Finally, we come to a stop outside of a small, well lit diner with a huge red fluorescent sign over it identifying this place to be Nora's. I still have my arm wrapped around Damien's waist when he quickly jumps off the bike, and I lose my balance slightly, causing me to tilt dangerously to the left. Luckily for me, Damien is like a freaking ninja and he grabs me and the bike before we both hit the ground. Using those beautiful biceps of his, he pulls my arm in sync with the bike so I'm straddling it again in an upright position.

The heat goes straight to my cheeks, and I refuse to meet his gaze. I can hear him choking back his laughter which only makes me blush more profusely. All alcohol that had been circulating through me back at the club has officially left my system. Oh, if only I was drunk right now, I really wouldn't mind this whole embarrass-ing-myself-in-front-of-a-really-hot-guy thing so much.

"Ace, please get off the bike. It is getting a little cold out here." Holding out his hand, Damien gives me a silent plea to hurry my ass up and get off his bike. I look at him to see him managing to keep a straight face, but his eyes give away the fact that he is still laughing on the inside. Grudgingly, I let him help me off the bike and lead me into the diner where he picks out the corner booth in the far corner away from the other two customers who don't acknowledge our presence even after we set off the little chime above to door.

Sliding in on the opposite side of the table, I study my surroundings in an attempt to ignore Damien so my cheeks—and let's face it, my whole body—can cool off for a bit. One look into those gorgeous green eyes, and I feel on fire. I make awkward eye contact with this middle aged woman who had been secretly staring at me, and here I was thinking the other customers didn't notice us show up. Not knowing what to do, I jerk my eyes away and focus on the red and black décor that covers the room—red vinyl seat covering, black and white tables, black and white checkered floors, black and red wall art.

An older lady, probably in her mid-forties, makes her way to our table armed with a coffee pot in her right hand, and two menus in her left. "How you kids doing tonight?" Her New York accent is thick, and the gum she is smacking on isn't helping it any. I make a noncommittal noise, but Damien brightens up at her presence.

"Hey May! Just got off work! How's your night going?" May regards him with a slow look of curiosity, and I can literally see the wheels click into place as she realizes she knows him.

"Damien, kid, hows are ya? Yous haven't been in here in forever!"

"I know. I've been really busy. This is the first time in a while I've gotten to work the first shift at the club without having to pull a double." I nod my head along with the conversation like I have some great knowledge of what they are talking about, but alas, I do not. Still, I'm going to pretend I do because judging by the looks May is sending my way, she thinks I'm some trashy whore he picked up at the club which is true, except for the trashy whore part, and he didn't pick me up in the sense that I'm going to sleep with him. He literally picked me up.

"What can I get yous guys?" She hadn't even given us a menu, and I am about to point this out when Damien interrupts me, claiming we both will have his usual. I squint my eyes at him to convey the fact that I do not approve of him ordering for me, but he either doesn't get my telepathic message or is just ignoring it. After a few more seconds of pleasantries that I'm not included in despite Damien's whole-hearted efforts, May walks off to give our order to the cook behind the counter.

"So, what did you just order me exactly?" Damien sends me a devilish smirk in response to my frown.

"My usual order."

"Thank you Sherlock. I was capable of figuring that out all by myself believe it or not." Damien's lip is twitching like mad, and it is obvious that he is doing everything in his power to not laugh at me right now. He is still trying to get his laughing under control, so he doesn't say anything else on the subject. Fine, two can play that game. His usual just better be a lot of food because I am famished. Looking out the window, I go into my own little world that I don't come out of until I feel a warm tingling starting at the back of my hand and spreading up my arm; Damien must be touching me again. Turning my eyes away from the window and to my hand, I find that I am right.

"Are you really mad that I ordered for you?" His voice comes out low and charming as hell. Add to the fact that he is doing this thing where he is looking at me from underneath his eyelashes while biting down on his bottom lip, and I am a complete puddle of nothing. I don't even remember the question right now. I'm too focused on that lip he keeps biting. I wish those were my teeth instead. I wonder how he would feel if I would kiss him right now. Would he find it too forward? I don't know. I do know that he needs to stop doing that though because it is distracting as hell.

"Are you staring at my lips?" I'm busted—big time. Lie! Which lie to tell, which lie to tell, which—wait! You have something in your teeth! No, he isn't showing his teeth. That would be completely stupid, and not believable. Come on Amanda, you can do this! You are not one of those dumb blonde cheerleaders. You are smart!

"No! Why would you think I was staring at your lips?" My voice comes out a little higher than my normal pitch, and it cracks half way through. It's official that I am the worst liar ever in the history of liars and lying games everywhere. Give me the crown because I am the King, or well Queen, of the worst liars. I demand a crown, and a throne, and a thing that thing that you hold that's like a stick. Wait just one minute. Maybe I am not as sober as I would like to think I am.

"You were! You want to kiss me!" He holds out the 's' in 'kiss' making it extra-long and snake like. Ugh, why can't I be a better liar? Well, they say honesty is the best policy! Here goes nothing.

"Yeah, so what if I do?" This takes Damien for a loop, and the shock is written all over his face. He recovers quite quickly though, but I think it is only because May brings us our food. He would probably argue that it was due to his amazing player skill, but whatever.

May walks away, leaving two feasts sitting in front of us. On my plate, I have a little mountain of eggs, bacon, and hash browns; and in a separate bowl, I have a lake of grits; and a small stack of pancakes tower on their own separate plate. I'm just about to dive in—fork poised to go and everything—when Damien clears his throat and leans over the table towards me. Being the person that I am, I lower my fork and lean forward a little. We sit just close enough to touch, but we don't. I'm silent for a few seconds, waiting for Damien to speak.

"Then, I think we should do something about it." It takes me a minute to realize that this is his response to what I said before May brought us our food. He is talking about us doing something about me wanting to kiss him. We are leaning closer and closer to each other, and now all I would have to do is lean forward another centimeter and our lips would be touching.

"Just not right now." He slams back into his booth and begins to shove food in his face. Half way through his plate of food, he stops long enough to give me a smirk for what, I don't know, but I don't care. There is something about him that makes me forget about the world around me. More importantly, I haven't really been dwelling on Cameron. There have been a few moments where I caught myself comparing the two guys, but where Cameron is all moody and mysterious, Damien seems to be fun and open; where Cameron is a total jackass, Damien seems like a nice guy who doesn't want to hurt me. The list goes on and on, and let me just say that it doesn't actually go in Cameron's favor. Except for the part where when Damien touches me it cannot compete to the way it feels when Cameron just grazes my skin. That's probably only because I just met him. If we kiss, I'm sure I'll feel that same electricity. I mean, I've been—no was—in love with Cameron for a very long time, and I just met Damien. Those type of feelings take time to progress. I can't just expect instant butterflies and feelings of utter happiness whenever he walks into a room when I've only ever been in two rooms with him.

Pushing those thoughts aside, I eat the eggs, pancakes, and bacon that Damien ordered, but I can't manage to eat through the hash browns and grits. It is way too much food, and here I was worried that there wouldn't be enough. If my dress zipper busts open, he is buying me a new dress because it is his fault that I ate so much. I couldn't turn all that delicious food down!

"I'm stuffed." I groan and lean back into my seat. There is no way I'm going to be able to move for a few minutes.

"But I don't remember doing anything, and trust me, you aren't the kind of girl I'd forget." Popping my head to the side, I give Damien a quizzical gaze in an attempt to get him to explain himself. He gives me a guilty smile.

"In England, 'I'm stuffed' means 'I just had sex.'" I feel the heat rise to my face, and Damien has a laugh at my expense while asking May to bring our check. I try to pull the money from my bra and hand it to him to pay for my share, but he pushes my money filled hand away.

"My treat Ace; your money isn't good here."

"Oh really? Where is it good then so I can repay you?"

"Sweetheart, it doesn't matter where you are. If I am there, your money will never be good."

A hundred watt grin makes its way to my face, and I can't help myself because that was one of the sweetest things I've ever heard in my life; I give Damien a quick peck on the cheek. In return, Damien gives me a back a smile to rival my own before getting up to pay the ticket. I follow wordlessly behind as he gives the money to May (leaving her a tip that exceeds the quality of service if I do say so myself) and heads back out to his bike.

"Have you ever driven one of these before?" Damien asks while motioning towards his bike.

"No, never." I don't like the look he has on his face as he climbs on his bike, not leaving me enough room to climb behind him.

"Damien scoot forward. I'm flattered that you think I'm that tiny, but I'm not." His only response is to scoot farther back and tap the space in front of him. Oh, hell no. I am not going to be driving this

two-wheeled death trap. It is safe when an experienced person is driving, but an un-experience, clumsy, spacey person—like me—should
not be allowed to drive this motorcycle, or any motorcycle for that
matter.

"Amanda, chill girl. I'm going to be pretty much doing everything.
You'll just be sitting in front of me with your hands on the bars." He
gives me an encouraging wave in response to my weary glare, but he
refuses to scoot forward. Well, if I'm not really driving, this can't be
that bad. Right?

Throwing my leg over in a way that I won't flash anyone within my
line of vision, I climb in front of Damien. I put my hands in the
appropriate location and wait for Damien to crank it or whatever
the motorcycle equivalent is. Suddenly, I feel Damien press himself
against my back, and I can feel every muscle in his body as he moves
his hands to start up the bike. I feel his hips shift into me slightly
as he kicks down on something, but I'm not focusing on that. I'm
focusing on the feeling I'm getting below the stomach if you get my
drift when he is pressing into me. To say I'm turned on is an understatement. I lean back into him slightly as we set off on the street, and
I can feel his breath caressing the back of my neck. The urge to turn
around and straddle the bike backwards is overcoming me in a not so
subtle fashion. Is this what he felt like when I was pressed up against
him because this is complete torture, and I apologize profusely for
doing that, even if it was an accident.

When we come to stop at a yellow light, I expect him to scoot back a little bit, but he doesn't. He moves closer if that is possible, resting his chin on my shoulder, and one of his hands on my outer thigh. I feel him begin to press small, barely there kisses along my shoulder and up my neck, stopping only to nibble on my ear. I close my eyes and tilt my head back slightly, not objecting to his hand moving to my inner thigh, making a small circular pattern well below the no-no leg zone but just high enough to turn me on like there is no tomorrow. Just like that though, he stops and the bike starts moving again. I'm not going to lie, it takes me a good few seconds to recover from what he just did to me, and he isn't turned on at all. Trust me, I would know because we are that close. Well fine, two can play that game.

Pushing my hips back a little, I move us closer if that is even possibly, but I don't move my hips. I just keep them there, during every bump, curve, and turn. I feel him tense slightly and let out a shallow growl, but I don't stop. I just keep pushing back into him, moving a bit more than necessary on the bumps until I can feel him moving under me. He is at full attention by the time we get to the next stop light which is when I decide it would be a good time to stop adjusting my seat, so I sit still again.

"I live in Sundown, so you need to take the right after next." I pass on the information like it is no big deal. It's not like we are messing with each other's hormones or anything on his bike. We are just going for a casual bike ride back to my place. Or that's what I'd like to believe when, Damien twists my body slightly so that I'm facing him. From the one look of lust on his face, I know what he is going to do before he does it. That's why I'm not surprised when his lips come crashing down on mine. Our tongues our dancing in a dangerous tango that ends all too soon when the light turns green and we our off again. I don't know what I'm doing. I'm not thinking this through at all. I should not be doing this with a guy I just met. I'm not a slut. It's just that when he touches me; I don't think, not at all.

Luckily for me, the next three lights are all green, and we make it into Sundown without having to stop again. I direct him down the intricate streets, and we come to a stop in front of my house where there are two cars waiting for me. Crap, I forgot Maria and Cameron are here, healing me back to "health." I scramble off the bike and Damien does the same. His happiness is even plainer now that we are standing up, and I feel a little guilty for doing that to him when I have no intention of doing anything else with him for a very long time, if ever.

"Goodnight Damien. Thanks for the ride." I go to walk away, but I stop when he wraps his arms around my waist, twisting me back into his chest.

"Can I come over sometime? Not to finish what we started, but to take you out on a real date at a real restaurant with real conversation. Trust me, tonight was not my finest of charming skills." He is smiling down at me, and I really respect him for leaving so much room between us, so I give him a quick peck on the lips in agreement. I should have known better because as soon as our lips connect, the peck is no longer innocent. I feel myself backing up the rest of the five feet to the door, and suddenly, my back is pressed against it due to the fact that Damien is pressed against me. His tongue laces into my mouth; and just as I realize we are going too far, the support on my back leaves suddenly, forcing Damien and I to tumble backwards.

"Thanks for bringing her home douchebag. You can leave now." I look up to see a very pissed off Cameron, hovering over us. When Damien doesn't get off me fast enough, Cameron grabs him by the neck of his shirt and throws him out the door. I hear him yell that he'll see me later, and then I hear the start of his bike, leaving me here alone to deal with Cameron.

Without a word to me, he closes the door and stomps off towards the living room. For some reason, I find that I'm lifting myself off the floor and following him in guilt and worry. As mad as I am still at him, I don't want him to be mad at me. That's one of the stupidest things I think I have ever thought. I shouldn't feel guilt over him being mad at me. I wasn't doing anything wrong. What making out with strangers is a crime now?

When I walk into the living room, I see Cameron pacing from one end of the room to another. If he doesn't slow down, he is going to wear down my carpet! I think I already see the line where he has been walking back and forth for a total of five seconds. What if I didn't come after him? He would have ruined my mother's rug! The inconsiderate jerk never thinks about anyone but himself.

"Stop it Cameron! Dammit! Why can't you ever think of anyone but yourself?"

This comment works: Cameron stops pacing. At the same time, it backfires on me because in three long strides he is standing in front of me, leaving only a few inches between us. I can see his chest heaving from his anger, and his eyes are like an angry sea before the storm. Instead of being turned on by this, I'm only more pissed off, and for some reason when I'm mad, I poke things. Slamming my finger into his chest, I step into him, forcing him to move back a little with every step.

"How dare you Cameron? How f*cking dare you? You don't get to act like a complete sweetheart one minute who seems to like kissing me to being a complete a**hole to being a sweetheart who brings me soup to being an a**hole who pisses me off." I accentuate the last three words with a jab to his chest for each one. I have officially backed him into a corner, and by the expression on his face, I do say I deserve a pat on the back. Looking into his eyes, I see I've gloated to soon because he looks ready to kill.

He takes a step forwards, forcing me to take a step back. Where I was control our movements before, he is controlling us now.

"How dare I? How dare you, Amanda? What you kissed one guy you suddenly have to go out and kiss them all?" With every word he said he took a step forward. While I was yelling and a tad out of control, Cameron is an ery calm that keeps me backing up: straight into a wall. Now, I have nowhere to go and am stuck, but Cameron doesn't stop. He keeps coming forward until our bodies are pressed together, bringing his face down level with mine. Even though he is in a fit of rage and I should be mad at him, my body deceives me yet again and begins to react to his close proximity. I can barely even focus on why I should be angry with him with him this close.

"Was I such a good kisser Amanda that it turned you into a slut who was willing to f*ck the first guy she came across who would have her?" Oh, right. Now I remember why I'm supposed to be mad at him—because he is an a**. Red comes over my vision, blinding my sight and judgement, and that is the reason my fist connects with that beautiful jaw line of his, sending him stumbling backwards a few inches. The punch would have been better if I could have truly gotten to swing at him, but I'll take what I can get!

Seeing him clutching his jaw sobers me up out of my fit of red hot anger, and I run to him and gently press my fingertips to his jaw.

"God Cameron, I didn't—I mean, I'm—."

"Don't you dare finish that thought."

"But, Cameron I just hit you!"

"I deserved in Panda. I deserve much worse." With one fleeting look, he makes his way to the couch and signals for me to sit next to him. Instead of doing what he asks, I situate myself on the coffee table in front of him and look at his face that is turning from a scary shade of red to a light purple already. I run my fingers over his jaw, and I can see him shudder. I hear him let out a low groan, so I pull my hand back suddenly so I won't cause him any more pain.

"How's your back?" I give him a look, showing my confusion.

"From where I made you fall earlier."

Oh, right. From where he pulled the door open so quickly, Damien and I—mid make out session—collapsed in on the floor. The memory of that embarrassing situation sends a blush to my cheeks, but I give him a little smile to communicate I'm okay.

"Intense Make-Out Rule Number Four: Don't do it against something that can move. Someone will get hurt." I laugh at Cameron's attempt at a joke, and I can feel us slowly slipping into the way things were before the whole bet incident.

I'm not sure how long we sit here just sitting in silence. It is nice to know he doesn't totally hate me for the way I acted, and let's face it: I never really hated him. He just hurt me to the point where I thought I did. Damien is nice, and he provided a much needed distraction tonight. He just isn't Cameron though, and that is probably the reason I did what I did next.

"How was I supposed to know? We never finished." Cameron looks at me with confusion splayed across his gorgeous face. His eyebrows are scrunched down over his eyes as if he were trying to read my thoughts so he could know what I am talking about.

"What?"

"How was I supposed to know about 'Intense Make-Out Rule Number Four'? We never finished Kissing School." Even though I really want to drop my gaze and crawl under the table to hide from the silence that surrounds us when the words leave my mouth, I don't. I sit there face to face with Cameron, refusing to drop my gaze.

"You do have a lot to learn."

"It would only make sense to continue."

"It would be a shame to let all that natural ability to go to waste."

"Would hate to not know what to do with it all."

"What lesson were we on again?"

Cameron and I have slowly leaned closer to each other so that I can feel his breath tickling my lips. I don't know why I'm such a masochistic person, but if that's what it takes to feel Cameron's lips against mine again, I'm willing to do it. Kissing Damien was nice, but it was just that: nice. Kissing Cameron is so much more than nice, and I don't want to give that up even if I am the one who gets hurt in the end.

"We are on lesson three."

"Ah right. Lesson three: make out sessions. They should be steamy, and when you pull away, you should want more. Don't give into that urge too soon though. Part of the fun is the wanting more.

Unfortunately, this isn't going to work. You need to be sitting next to me on the couch."

Following his advice, I reluctantly move away from the close proximity of his lips and sit on the couch next to him. He leans back, giving me a smirk.

"Okay. Let's set the scene: you're with some guy and you're watching a movie at your house. You guys are the only ones home, and it is going to stay that way for a while. Casually, he lifts his arm up, wraps it around you, and begins playing with your hair. What do you do?"

I look downward and smirk before turning slightly in the arm that Cameron had wrapped around his shoulder. I look up under my eye lashes at him, making it obvious that I'm looking between his eyes and lips which are slowly lifting up at the corners into a smile; but I don't have to wait long before they are leaning towards me and connecting with my own lips. At first the kiss starts off slow, with just a slight peck, but this is a make out session lesson after all. Cameron nips at my bottom lip asking for entrance, and I willingly comply.

It doesn't take long before he has pushed me down on the couch and moved on top of me. I don't know how he is doing it, but I feel on fire just from the touch of his lips. His hands roam down my sides, but they never stray into the "no-no zone." I thank him silently all the while cursing him because as much as I want to wait, I want to keep going, but we don't. We just lay there making out. After what feels like a few minutes, Cameron pulls away and stands up from the couch, pulling me up with him.

"Well, that was a relatively short lesson." I say while we are heading upstairs towards our bedrooms with a fair amount of distance between us, signifying that there will be no more lessons tonight.

"Panda, do you know what time it is?" I look around me, but there are no devices sitting around waiting to tell me the time anywhere. Well, let's see. I think I left the club with Damien around midnight, putting us home around one.

"1:30?" Cameron stops in front of my bedroom door and laughs.

"Try more like four a.m. We have been making out for almost three hours now." I let my mouth fall open in shock because right now I don't care if it is lady-like or not.

"No! That didn't feel like three hours!" Cameron shakes his head and begins stepping backwards towards the guest bedroom where he has been staying.

"Time flies when you're having fun. Night Panda." Closing the door behind him, Cameron steps into the bedroom, leaving me alone in the hall. I just made-out with him for three hours, and I'll be damned if they weren't the best three hours of my life. Glad to see I'm not regretting my decision to set myself up for heartbreak just yet. Going to bed, I lie there in anticipation of what adventures tomorrow will bring. Hopefully, lesson four will be one of them.

Chapter 9--Be careful, or Else You'll Get an ImproperLesson on PDA

C hapter 9

My whole body is shaking, and I am slowly jerked out of my wonderful dream of being a rock star. Instead of fans screaming my name and professing their love for me, Maria is screaming my name professing her annoyance of how I won't get my butt out of bed. I push her off of me slightly and attempt to roll back over, but she won't have any of that. She is persistent that one. Sometimes, like early in the morning, I question our friendship.

"Go away Maria!"

"No! You are going to school today, so wake up!" Maria gives me a final shove, sending me toppling onto the ground next to my bed. That's it! I'm going to crucify this girl for interrupting my sleep, but

before I can wrap my fingers around her neck, she is out of the room
and down the stairs. That's fine, but I will be plotting my revenge on
her later today. Since I'm up already, I make my way to the shower
and begin to get ready for the day.

The whole process is taking longer than usual because I keep re-play-
ing last night over and over in my head. Damien was fun, but
Cameron was, well, Cameron. How could Damien even begin to
compete with perfection like that? I mean that hair, and those lips,
and the way it feels when he is kissing me—Damien just isn't quite up
to par. However, I care for Cameron a lot; and that is scary because
I don't think he feels the same way. I'm risking everything again,
practically setting myself up for heartbreak. The smart girl in me
should be saying, "No! Don't do it! He is a player! Just say no!"
Unfortunately, the love-sick, hormonal teenager in me is shutting her
up quite efficiently.

Maria's angry voice radiates up the stairs signaling that I need to get
a move on or else face serious consequences. I spray one final spritz
of perfume before grabbing my backpack and heading downstairs to
meet Maria who greets me with a wolf-whistle.

"Well, I'll be damned. Amanda, if I do say so myself, you are one sexy
b-otch!" I just laugh at her as I follow her out of the house towards
her car. Cameron's car is gone this morning, but that doesn't surprise
me because we are running fifteen minutes late. We are going to have
to break all sorts of speed limits in order to get to school in time.
Luck for us, Maria is driving. Getting there in less than ten minutes

shouldn't be a problem at all. Now, I'll just have to close my eyes and spend the next ten minutes of my life praying for safety!

I feel the car lurch to a stop, but I still refuse to peel open my eyelids. If it is even possible, I think her driving abilities are getting worse with time, and people say things get better with time! Lies! I flounder around for the handle bar, grasping onto its cool metal and plunging out of the car. Finally, I open my eyes only to be momentarily blinded by the natural light. Some of my fellow cheerleaders are hanging out under a tree, and they wave at me, beckoning me to come over. I wave politely back, but I stick with Maria and head towards her brother. I can see her tensing when she realizes I'm following her, but I give her a reassuring smile that hopefully says, "It's okay. I'm over him." Instead of "It's okay. We hooked up last night." I really hope she doesn't get the second message.

"Hey Cameron!" Maria's voice is strained, but I can hear an underlying tone of excitement. She loves Cameron to death, and she is trying to hate him for my benefit. Unfortunately, she can't stay mad at him for long, so she is putting on an act now, trying to seem like she is still mad.

"Hey sis, Panda." I nod my head at him, but I don't say anything. I'm still supposed to be heartbroken after all. I shouldn't feel too comfortable in his presence just yet, or else Maria might be suspicious. Maria opens her mouth to say something, but she is cut off by the loud squeal of the bell indicating that it was time to head to class. A look of complete horror crosses her face, and she runs off, mumbling something about a history assignment behind us. Now, Cameron and I are completely alone, but at least I don't have to fake silence because I have no idea what to say. Lucky for me, Cameron breaks the tension when he pulls out an energy drink from his backpack and wordlessly hands it to me. I give him a questioning look, but he doesn't say anything. He just looks right back at me before beginning to move towards class, and just as I think I won't get an explanation, he steps into me, pressing my body deadly close against his.

"Drink up Panda. You'll need your energy for lesson four this afternoon."

With those words, he was off to class as if he wasn't just pressed up against me in a very non-friendly way. I steal a look around, trying to see if anyone witnessed our little encounter. Luck was on my side again because no one else was outside which is good, but it also means I'm going to be late for class.

Just like I predicted, I walked into first period after the tardy bell rang, and because my teacher is the wonderful human being she is, she sent me directly to the office to get my late slip. That's how my morning started off, and it didn't get much better until now because it is now lunch time. Let's face it. That is every single high school student's favorite part of the day. Freshmen, sophomore, junior, or senior—it doesn't matter. Everyone loves lunch.

I walk in and try to spot Maria, but I don't see her little head anywhere, meaning I'm here first. Sweet victory! That means I get to get the yummy food—none of that healthy crap she likes. When I reach the line, I find that not only do we have pizza (my favorite!) but also nachos and fries. I feel like a complete pig as I pile my tray up, but I don't care. I'll run it off later. I don't question my choice to grab dessert when I see that it is chocolate chip cookies. Well, that is until I hear a low chuckle erupting from behind me as I slide four cookies onto my tray. Whipping around, I'm face to face with Cameron.

"Forget Panda. I think I will dub thee cookie monster." Being the mature adult that I am, my response is to stick my tongue out at him. My come-backs are monumental, I swear. He gives me a devilish smirk and steps in closer to me.

"Be careful Panda. I might have to give you an impromptu lesson on PDA if you keep tempting me with your tongue." His words are low and husky, and they make a blush spread up over my cheeks, making him bend over in laughter. It isn't till after my whole face has turned red that I realize that he is yet again just teasing me. Before I can retort with something, the cashier calls me up to pay; but before I can get my money out, Cameron hands her a twenty, indicating he wants to pay for us both.

"Cameron, I can get my own lunch."

"Please, that is half for my sister, and you know it. Let me play the good guy every once in a while Panda." The lunch lady's eyes go all doe-like, and she lets out a low 'awe' since he is just so adorable. I can't help but to roll my eyes at her reaction. He chuckles, giving her a wink before steering us out of the line. I'm about to walk away before he grabs my elbow and places his lips against my ear.

"Lesson today at six at the factory." I feel his warm breath leave my skin, leaving me standing there momentarily dazed. I physically have to shake myself before walking over to our table where I am forced to meet Maria's questioning gaze, but she doesn't vocalize any concern. Instead, she dives straight into the food. I'm thoroughly enjoying my daydream continuation about my dream of being a rock star from the night before when Maria's voice breaks through the silencel.

"Isn't that that hot bouncer from the club?" Whipping my head around, I see Damien standing in the door way of the cafeteria, silently scanning over all the tables which are all focused on him. He spots me and gives me a slight wave before heading towards our table.

"Hold up one second missy!" Maria's voice cuts through the air, but at a volume only we can hear.

"You failed to tell me about your hottie encounter last night!"

"Well, I didn't think about it this morning, but I'll tell you about it later." She is about to protest, but Damien steps up the table, forcing her to drop whatever argument she was about to make.

"Hey beautiful, so I was thinking: would you like to go out on a date with me tonight? I know it is late notice, but it is my only night off for a couple of days. I don't want to have to wait a couple of days before seeing your face again." His words send a blush to my cheeks, and I am about to say yes when I catch Cameron's heated gaze. Shit, Cameron. What the hell am I going to do?

Chapter 10--Kissing School is Still in Session, Whether You Like It or Not

----

C hapter 10

I open my mouth to say something, but no words are coming out. Instead, I sit with my mouth agape, staring at Damien. I'm sure I look like an utter idiot, but I can't seem to fix my situation. Damien wants to go out tonight and part of me wants to go with him, but I already made plans with Cameron. However, it isn't like Cameron and I are going out on a date; we are just having one of our "lessons." Would it be in bad taste to cancel on him? Do I even want to? The idea of getting to kiss Cameron again sends me into a blushing fit which tells me exacly who it is that I really want to be with tonight.

"I'm sorry Damien, but I already made plans with Maria tonight." His face falls visibly when I turn him down, and I had no intention of trying to reschedule our date. Well, that was until he looked so sad when I turned him down.

"Maybe I can come visit you at the club this weekend, and we can get together the next time you have off?" The words are out of my mouth long before I wish to take them back.

"That'd be great! I'm off not next Saturday. Would that be okay?" Nodding my head, I agree to that date, and with a final smile, Damien leaves me and Maria alone.

She gives me a look and is about to rip into when the bell rings for us to go to our next class. I don't hesitate to jump up from my seat and practically run out of the cafeteria, leaving both Maria and Cameron calling after me. As much as I love them both, I really don't feel like answering their questions about Damien right now. I don't even know the answers yet, so how am I supposed to tell them?

Slinking out the side entrance, I manage to make it out of the school building without anyone noticing. I set off toward the football field, crawling under the bleachers when I get there. Lowering myself against the cool metal pillars, I slide down onto the hard dirt flooring. This is such a mess. I swear. If it weren't for Cameron, I would probably still be with some sweetheart of guy who I really liked. That never happened though because I was too busy being in love with Cameron to ever fall for someone else. Hell! It is even his fault that

I met Damien! If it weren't for him being such a jerk, I would never have gone to the club and been so daring!

"Panda?" Cameron's frame comes into my vision has he ducks under the bleachers, towering over me. He gives me a hesitant look before sliding down onto the ground next to me. I look at him, but do not respond. He knew I wanted to be alone. That's why I am out here, yet he follows me anyways. If he wants to talk, then he can talk. That doesn't mean that I have to be doing all of it.

"That was the guy? The one who you, um, you, that you were..." He looks at me, pleading to not make him go on, but I sit silently waiting for him to finish his question.

"That was the guy who brought you home?" I nod my head yes.

"Did he ask you out today?" Again, I nod my head yes.

"Oh." He drops his head, hiding his face from my view. We sit in silence for a few moments with me just watching his downturned face.

"Did you say yes?" His voice is barely above a whisper as it wafts up from his down-turned face. Once again, I nod my head yes, but it dawns on me that he can't see me nodding my head.

"He asked me out for tonight, but I said no. I told him next Friday." Cameron turns to look at me, and I can see conflict in his eyes. I'm not sure why, but a terrible feeling seeps into every inch of my pores.

"You should have said yes Amanda. You should have blown me off."
Cameron's face is set in a hard line, and I cannot look away no matter
how hard I want to. Even when the tears start to well up in my eyes,
I cannot look away from his face.

"I could never—."

"I know Amanda. You could never do that to me because you love
me." How did he know that? He knows I'm in love with him. My
jaw hands open as I stare at him in shock.

"Cameron—." His hand comes up and covers my mouth.

"Look Panda, I know you love me okay? I've known it for a long time,
but you have to hear me when I say I'm no good for you. There are
things about my past that Maria has kept from you. Hell, there are
things from my past that I've kept from Maria. I don't known this
kid, but he seems like a decent guy. Don't put off a chance at being
with him because you think you have a chance at being with me.
I'm not looking for a relationship with you Amanda. This is purely
physical for me." His voice is so strained at the end, and I can see
why. It isn't like it would be easy to tell a girl who is in love with you
that there will never be anything more than a physical relationship
between the two of you. He is right. I can't blow of Damien just
because of Cameron anymore. However, if he thinks that I'm just
going to admit that this is anything more than physical to me, he is
wrong on so many different levels.

"Cameron, that's sweet, but I never wanted anything from this other than make-out lessons which you have so dutifully given me. I would like to continue them because I have a feeling Damien is much more experienced than me in the field of sex."

"Sex! Who in the f***k said anything about sex?" Cameron's once passive face is now filled with anger. Can you say bi-polar much?

"I'm going to have sex one day Cameron, and that one day might be with Damien. You never know, but I want to continue Kissing School so that I can know what to do. Especially if it comes down to you know, doing it." Standing up, I begin to walk off, leaving a still disgruntled looking Cameron under the bleachers, but I stop half way.

"Kissing School is still in session Cameron. Be at the factory, and don't make me wait."

I'm not sure what just came over me, making me so in control and bossy, but I think I like this girl. Especially since this girl has just decided to make Cameron fall for her whether he likes it or not.